# BOO!

## Ros Asquith

## Illustrated by Andi Good

Collins

An imprint of HarperCollinsPublishers

My mum said to me today,
"You silly little moose!
You're so shy, you wouldn't say,
'**BOO!**' to a goose."

"Well," I thought, "I could...
If I saw a goose, I would."

Instead...

I saw a **monster**

But it didn't see me.

I crept up right behind it,
And shouted, noisily...

BOO!

But the monster wasn't frightened.
It didn't seem to care.
It just danced around in circles,
As if I wasn't there.

Then I found a
**tiger** -

Or I thought I had,
at least -

So I sneaked up softly to the huge, **FEARSOME** beast...

BOO!

It was very, very scary,
As I might have been his tea,
But the tiger wasn't fierce at all –
He came and purred at me.

Soon I saw a great big **bear**
But he didn't frighten me!
I stood quite still in front of him
And yelled, **ferociously...**

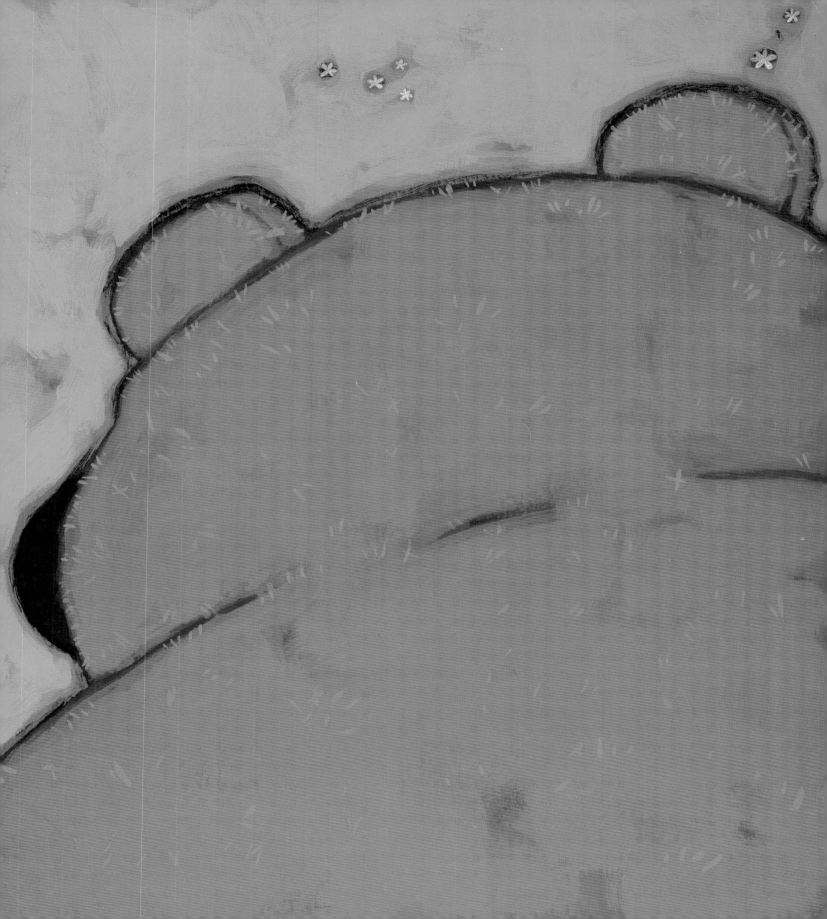

# BOO!

But the bear hardly noticed me –
He showed no sign of fear.
So I gave him a cuddle
And he grinned from ear to ear.

Next I met some pirates
With flags and chains and knives.
I thought, "I'll make these pirates
All run for their lives!"

BOO!

I really scared those pirates!
They vanished right away!
Shame – I would have liked it
If a pirate came to play.

So when I saw some **COWBOYS**
Galloping away,
I didn't say "**BOO!**" - I said,
"Please stay! Can I play?"

But they said,

"**GO AWAY!**"

"Don't be sad," my mum told me,
"You've been so brave today.
The cowboys didn't mean it.
They're asking you to play.

Now you deserve a small surprise.
Guess what I have for you?"
I hoped that it would be a goose
So I could call him...

BOO!

# Every child deserves the best...

0-00-664627-1

0-00-715002-4

0-00-710794-3

0-00-713728-1

0-00-664775-8

0-00-710624-6

0-00-664777-4

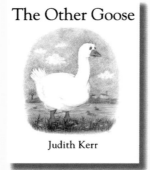

0-00-712735-9

0-00-714011-8

0-00-664728-6

Collins

*An imprint of HarperCollinsPublishers*